WITHDRAWN

Damaged, Obsolete, or Surplus
Jackson County Library Services

Jackson

County

Library

System

OCT 1 1 1994

HEADQUARTERS:

413 W. Main

Medford, Oregon 97501

GAYLORD M2G

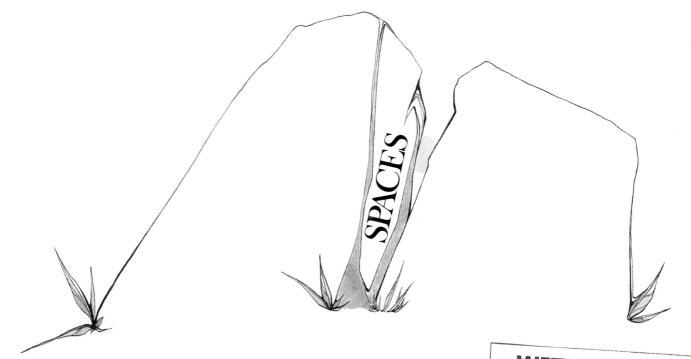

SPACES

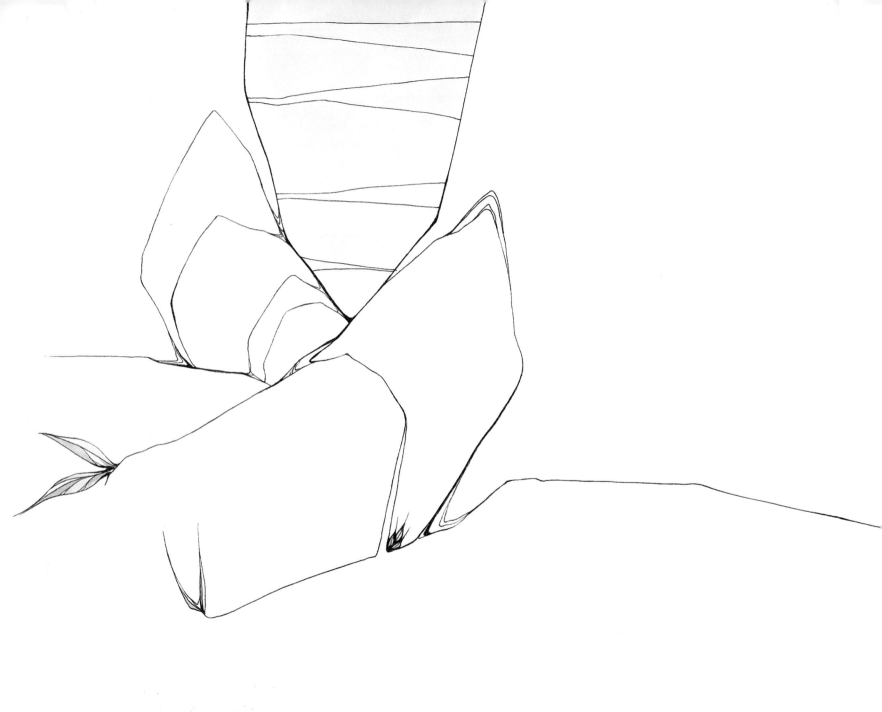

SPACES

WRITTEN AND ILLUSTRATED BY
PETER PARNALL

The Millbrook Press
Brookfield, Connecticut

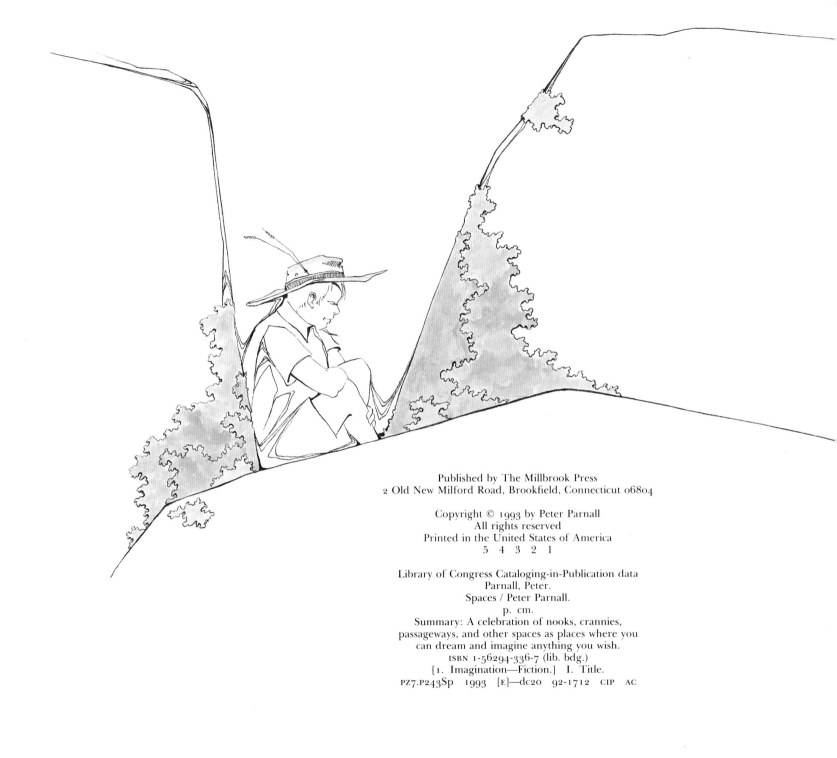

Published by The Millbrook Press
2 Old New Milford Road, Brookfield, Connecticut 06804

Library of Congress Cataloging-in-Publication data
Parnall, Peter.
Spaces / Peter Parnall.
p. cm.
Summary: A celebration of nooks, crannies,
passageways, and other spaces as places where you
can dream and imagine anything you wish.
ISBN 1-56294-336-7 (lib. bdg.)
[1. Imagination—Fiction.] I. Title.
PZ7.P243Sp 1993 [E]—dc20 92-1712 CIP AC

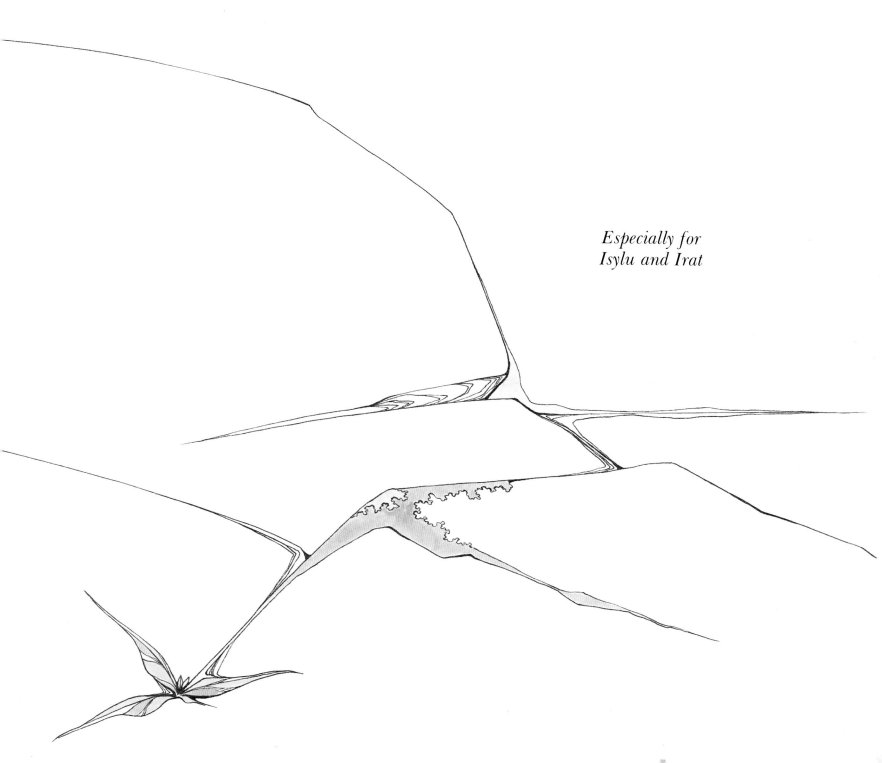

*Especially for
Isylu and Irat*

Some people think spaces are empty places. Places between more important things, things that you can touch. Things you can see.

Some are big. Some are as small as a gap in an old rock wall . . . no elbow room there. But then, a family of elephants doesn't *need* much room, if they are as small as your mind can make them!

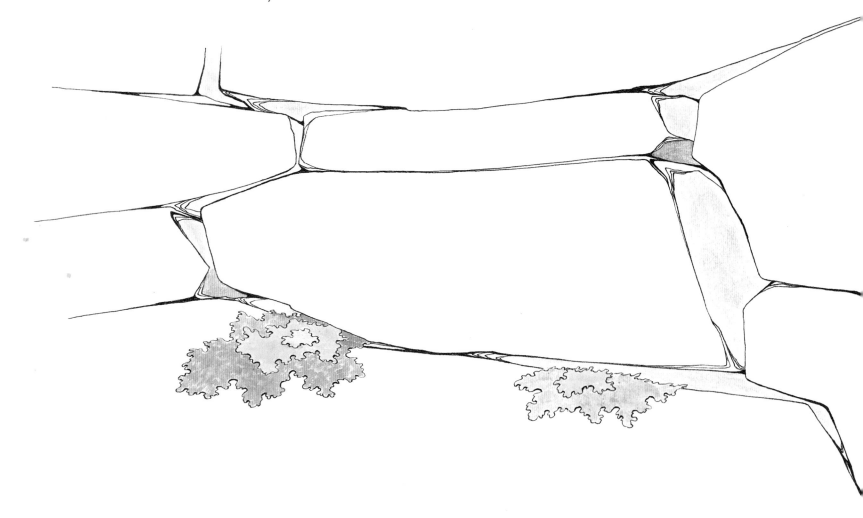

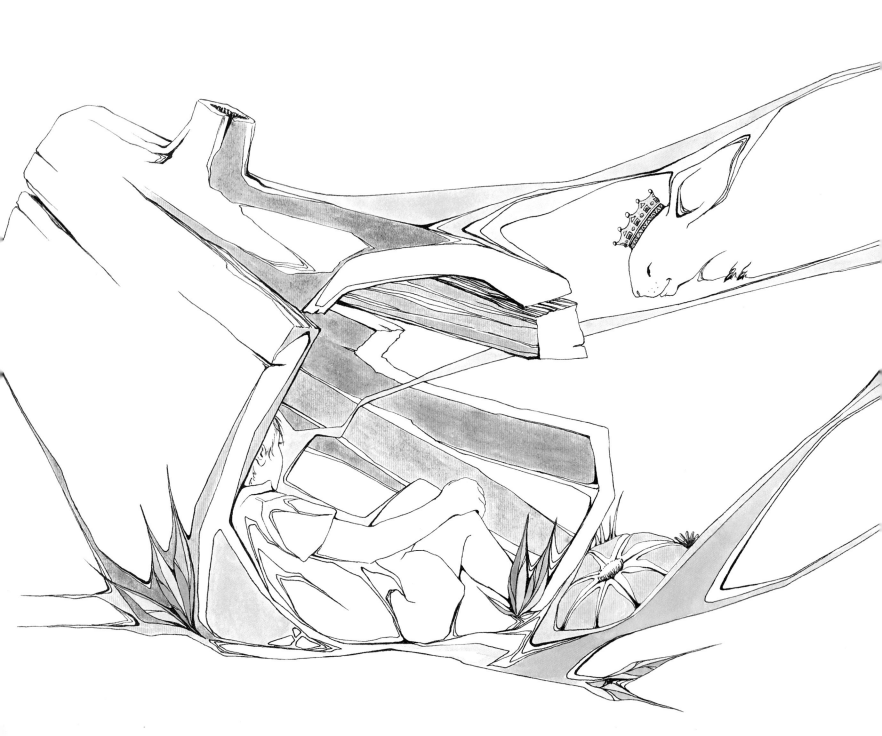

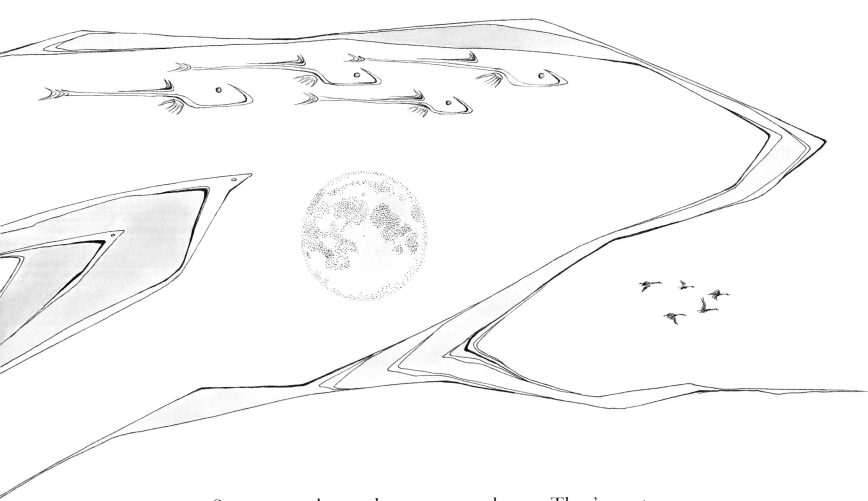

Spaces are places where you can dream. They're not empty, or something left over because no one thought of what to put there.

Dreams can soar as far in a hollow log as they can in the limitless space between the stars.

My friends think the cramped crawl space beneath our barn is a wasted place . . . just a musty den full of cobwebs and discarded things that never quite reached the dump.

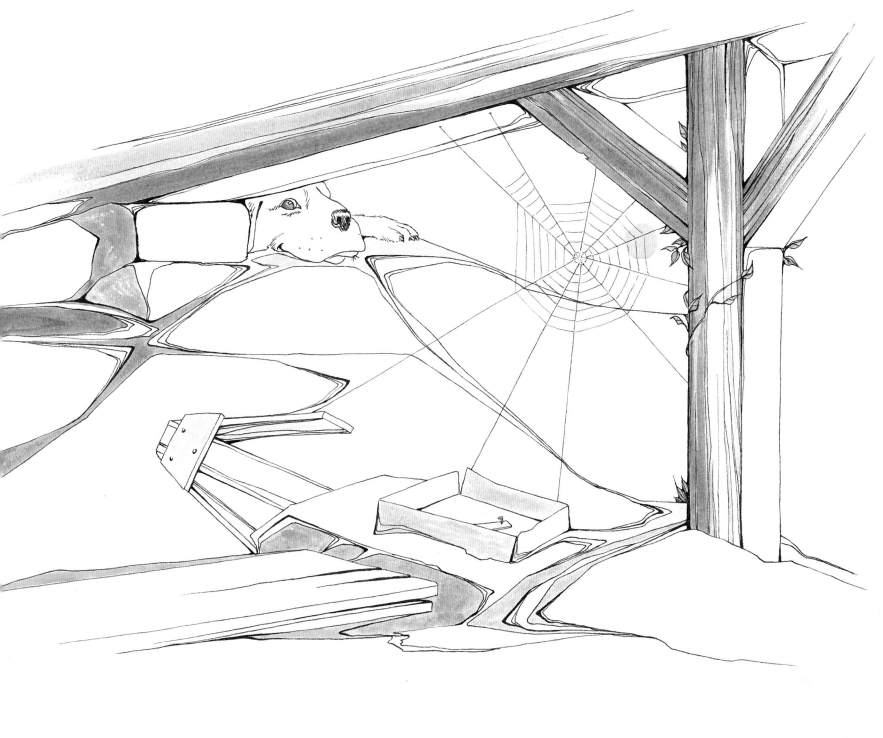

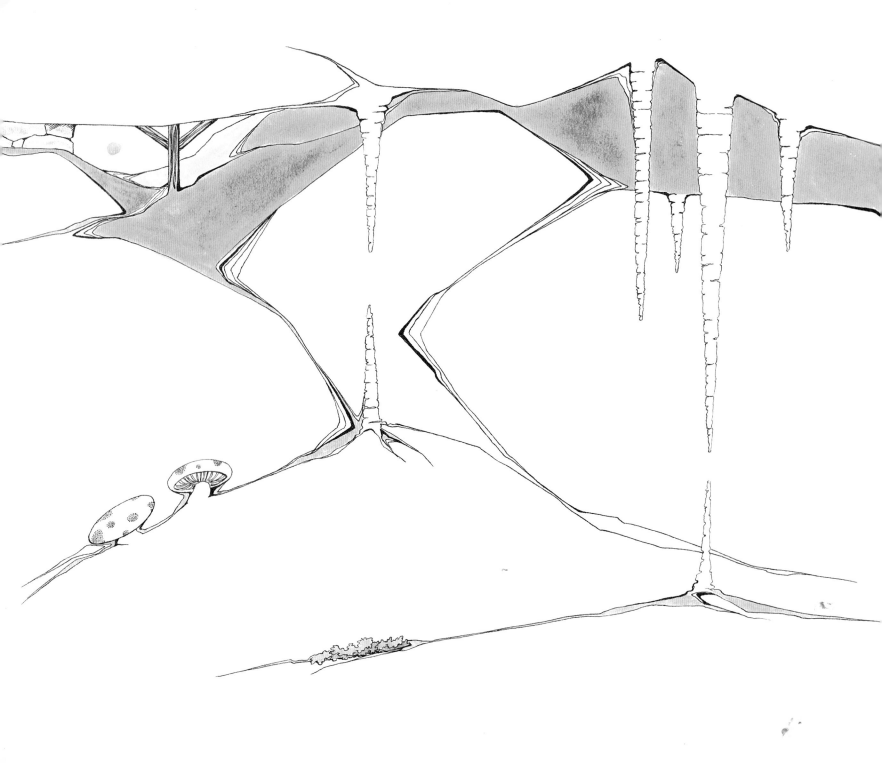

It is really a mammoth cave to explore. You might even discover hidden treasures, unseen since ancient times.

Way down, down in the deepest shadows of your mind, beyond the tightest tunnels the cavern has to offer, are spaces that store memories. One of mine is how the kitchen smelled on a baking day.

And kittens.
All the kittens loved to snooze in the tight, warm
space between the floor and a wood-fired kitchen stove.

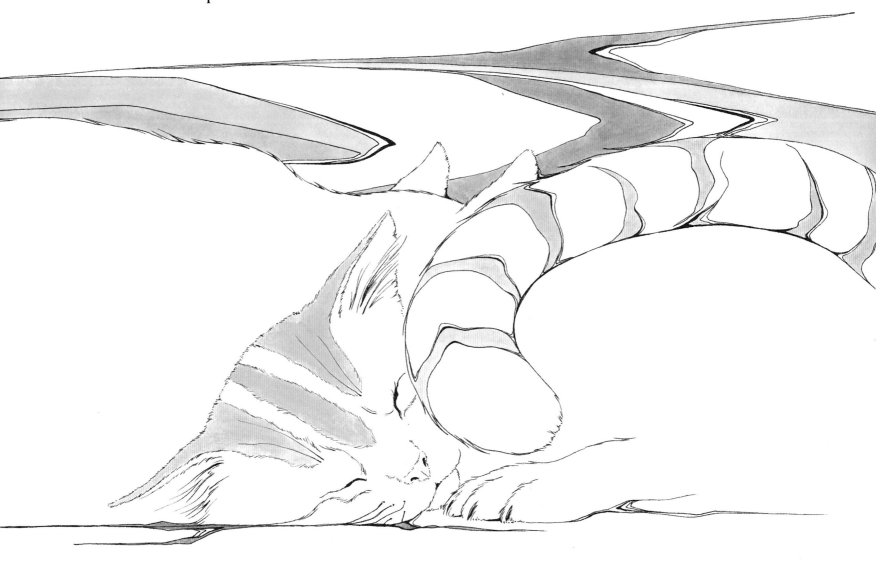

If not kittens, then perhaps that space would be a
perfect place for storing a fine collection of dragons
until summer sun arrives to warm their bones . . .
or maybe tigers.

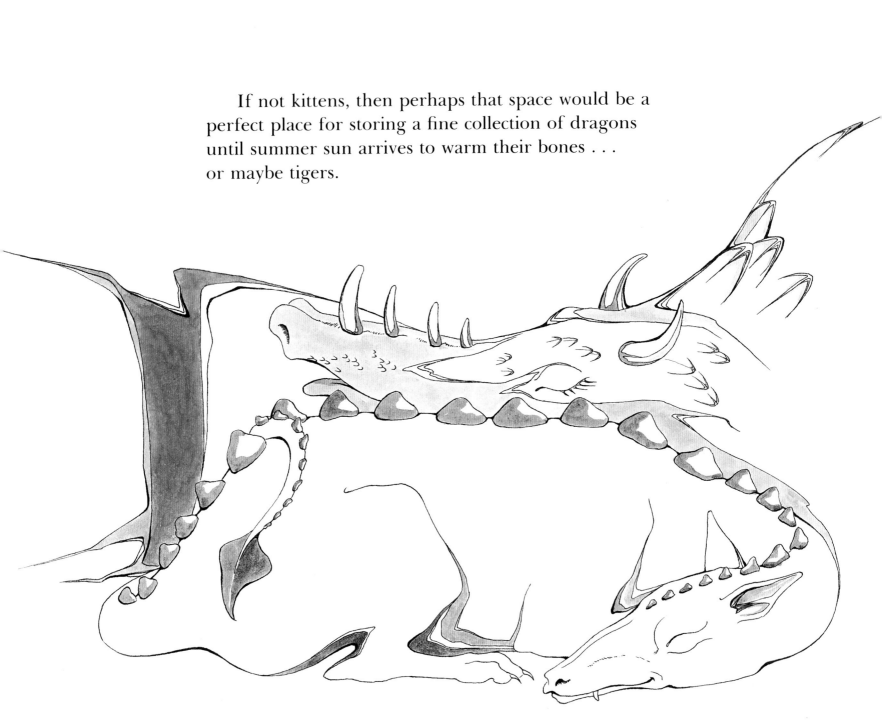

But then, tigers are usually under the dining-room table.
You can spend hours there practicing spine-tingling roars
and planning evening hunts for the biggest game the jungle
hides in its gloomy, dangerous depths.

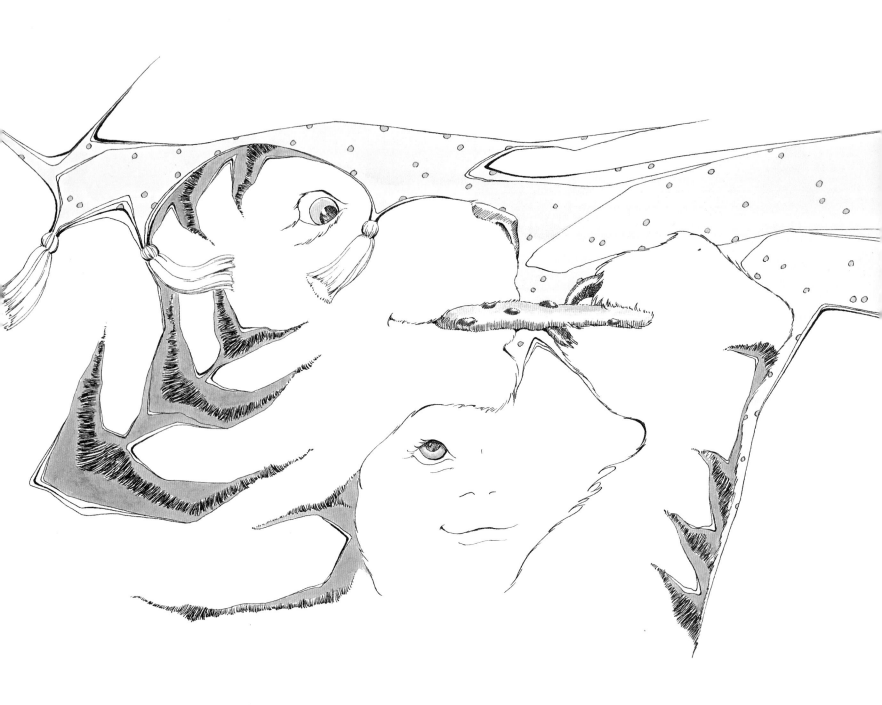

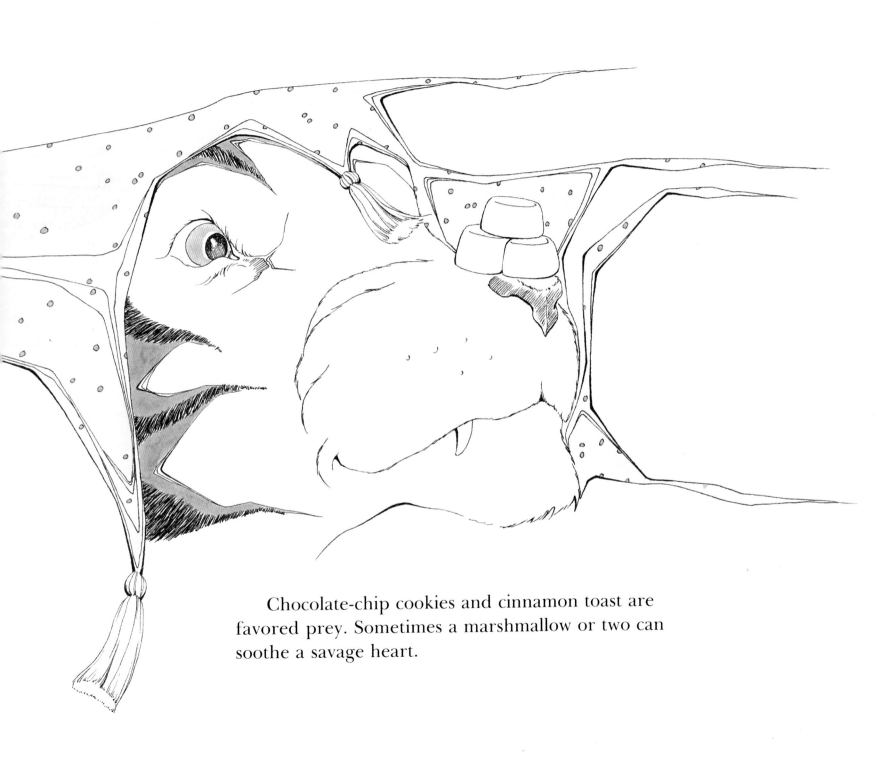

Chocolate-chip cookies and cinnamon toast are favored prey. Sometimes a marshmallow or two can soothe a savage heart.

Deep in the cramped passageways of a stove-wood pile, armored knights might stand in a row, guarding other spaces far within and deep below from prying eyes and probing hands.

Maybe there is a throne room there, or a ballroom full of waltzing mice!

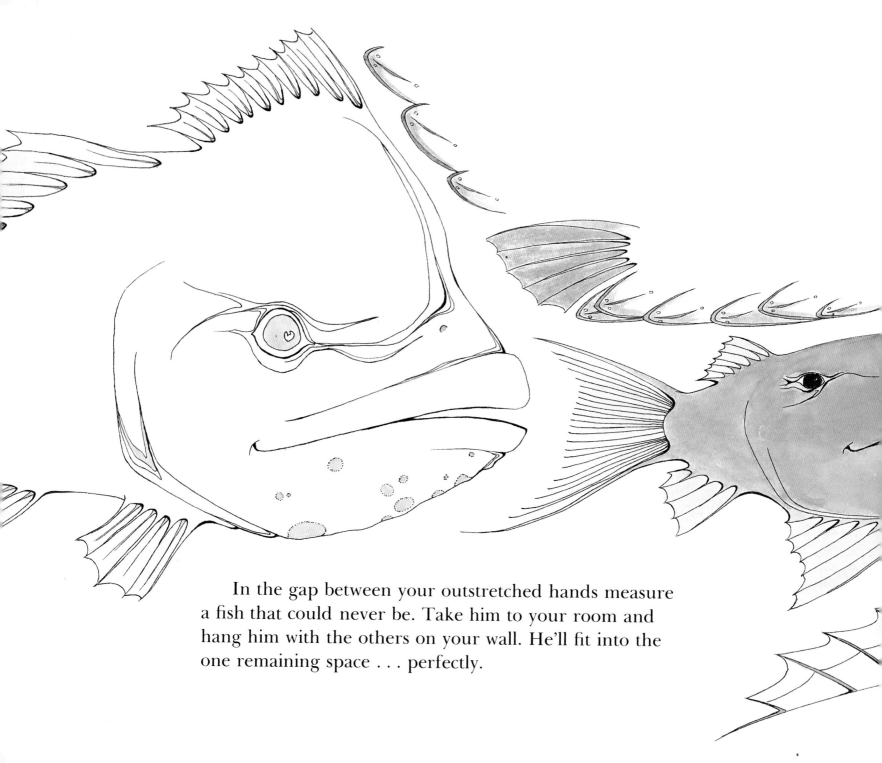

In the gap between your outstretched hands measure a fish that could never be. Take him to your room and hang him with the others on your wall. He'll fit into the one remaining space . . . perfectly.

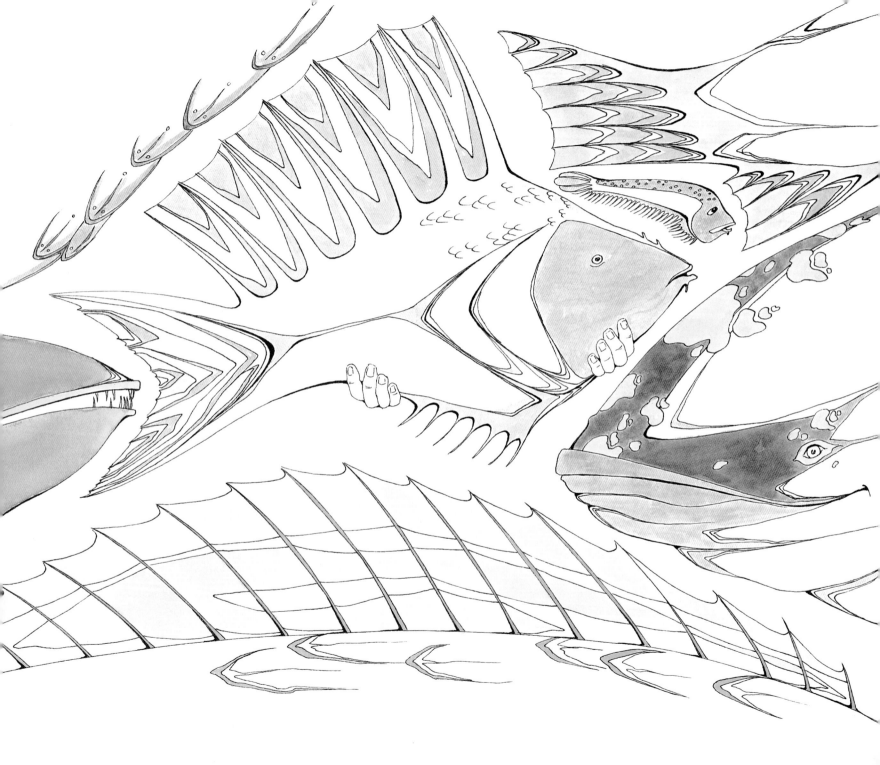

A tall space between bales of hay and the storeroom
wall could be an ice crevasse in far Tibet. When you
climb to the top you might see past China, across
Japan, to an island in the far South Seas.

You could talk to a shipwrecked sailor,
left over from whaling days.

In all places there are spaces . . . nooks and crannies,
holes and slots, passageways waiting . . . for you to fill
them with your own kinds of make-believe.

I love spaces. Last night I was wondering how many
wild horses would fit between the sunset and a distant
line of darkened trees.

As many as you want, I'll bet.